When Mary Ann and Louie complain about the cold, Grandpa tells them about the cold weather of *his* childhood. One morning he and Wainey took the dog for a walk. It was so icy that at the end of the day they were still in exactly the same place. Soon snow covered all the houses. Somehow Grandpa and Wainey found themselves inside a giant snowball. . . . This bubbling adventure will melt the coldest heart, as America's favorite Grandpa once again does a gentle snow job on his grandchildren.

JAMES STEVENSON

'BRRR!

GREENWILLOW BOOKS, New York

Watercolor paints and a black pen
were used for the full-color art.
The text type is ITC Clearface.

Copyright © 1991
by James Stevenson
All rights reserved.
No part of this book
may be reproduced or
utilized in any form
or by any means,
electronic or mechanical,
including photocopying,
recording, or by any
information storage
and retrieval system,
without permission in
writing from the Publisher,
Greenwillow Books,
a division of William
Morrow & Company, Inc.,
1350 Avenue of the Americas,
New York, NY 10019.

Printed in Hong Kong by
South China Printing
Company (1988) Ltd.
First Edition
10 9 8 7 6 5 4 3 2 1

Library of Congress
Cataloging-in-Publication Data
Stevenson, James (date)
Brrr! / James Stevenson.
    p.   cm.
    Summary: When Mary Ann and
Louie complain about the cold and
snow, Grandpa tells them about
the really cold winter of 1908.
    ISBN 0-688-09210-1.
    ISBN 0-688-09211-X (lib. bdg.)
    [1. Grandfathers—Fiction.
2. Winter—Fiction.
3. Snow—Fiction.
4. Cartoons and comics.]
I. Title.
PZ7.S84748Sn   1991
[E]—dc20
89-34615   CIP   AC

"Cold!" said Grandpa. "When my little brother Wainey sneezed, his sneeze *froze*."

"I remember Wainey taking a hot bath to get warm.
Unfortunately, the window was open a crack....

A few minutes later, Wainey *and* his bath had to be
lifted out of the bathtub and allowed to melt."

"One morning," said Grandpa, "we started to take the dog for a walk. But it was so icy that at the end of the day we were still in exactly the same place."

"Wainey and I went sledding on
a hill that had a tree on top.

Soon the tree was half
buried in snow.

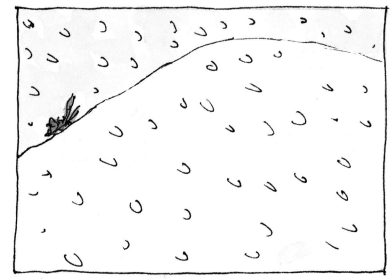

When the tree disappeared entirely,
we knew it was time to head home.

But by then the town had disappeared, too."

"Wainey was sliding down the hill.

I began to slide after him.

I heard soft, lovely music....

Wainey's head was hitting icicles as he slid past a barn.

We headed straight for Farmer Manning's clothesline."

"And along came…

a gust of wind.

We floated over the town to a big hill."

"...a herd of deer.

The deer began to run, and I fell off.

I searched for Wainey.

He wasn't hard to find.

I tried to cheer him up....

I built a big snowman,

but it began to fall over.

It turned into a giant snowball,

and got bigger and bigger as it went downhill, heading for our village.

The snowball rolled down Elm Street, uncovering one house after another…

and then it came to a stop."

The ice began to crack and shatter.

Then all the ice fell off the house.
Our parents came out and greeted us.

Wainey ran down the street, de-icing
ail the other houses."

"Our house, and all the other houses, were completely covered with ice."

"I whispered something to Wainey....

Wainey let out an ear-splitting cry!